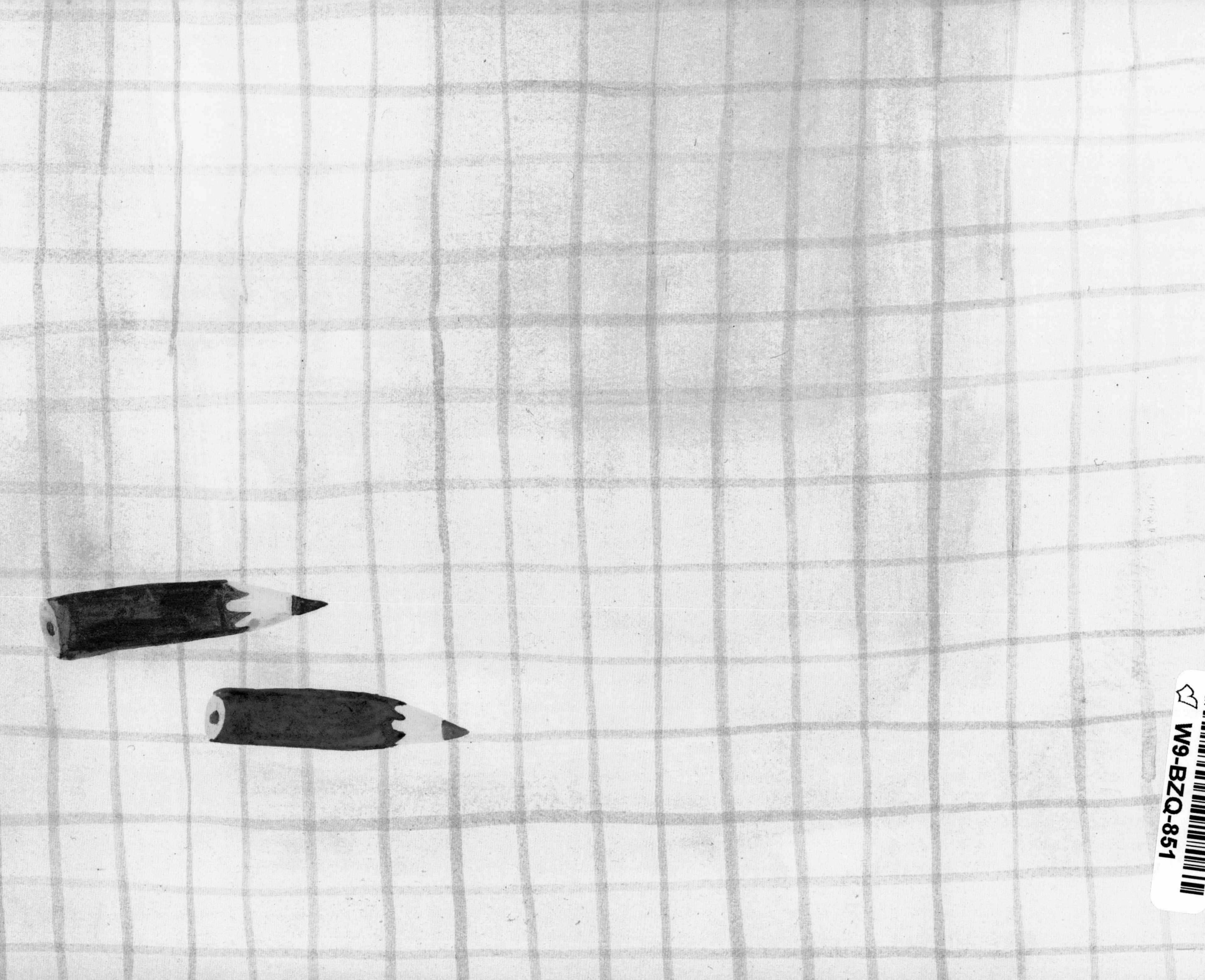

W9-BZQ-851

Davide Cali is an award-winning children's book author and cartoonist. He has written many popular children's books published in twenty-five countries.

Maria Dek creates original and expressive watercolor illustrations from her home in Białowieża, Poland, a village in the oldest forest in Europe. She holds degrees from the Academy of Fine Arts in Warsaw and University of the Arts London.

For Julek—my Little Explorer.

—M.D.

For Maria and Julian.

—D.C.

Published by
Princeton Architectural Press
202 Warren Street
Hudson, New York 12534
www.papress.com

Printed and bound in China
24 23 22 21 4 3 2 1 First edition

Published by arrangement with Debbie Bibo Agency

ISBN 978-1-61689-937-0

This book was illustrated using watercolors.

Translated from the Italian by Debbie Bibo
Book design by Orith Kolodny

For Princeton Architectural Press:
Editor: Parker Menzimer
Typesetting: Natalie Snodgrass

Library of Congress Cataloging-in-Publication Data
available upon request.

WHERE THE WORLD ENDS

DAVIDE CALI | MARIA DEK

A Zip, Trik, and Flip Adventure

Princeton Architectural Press | New York

It was a sunny and sleepy afternoon. Zip, Trik, and Flip had nothing to do but stare at the passing clouds.

"Where do the clouds go when we can't see them anymore?" asked Zip.

"Who knows," said Trik.

"Maybe they wind up where the world ends," said Flip.

"Where's that?" asked Zip.
"I don't know," answered Flip. "But I guess you'd just have to walk straight ahead to find out..."

Off the three friends went, to find the end of the world.

"We can always ask for directions along the way," said Zip.
"I'll bring the peanuts!" said Flip.

"Excuse me, can you tell us where the world ends?" Zip asked a shopkeeper at the edge of town.

"Not here, that's for sure," the shopkeeper replied.

"The end of the world? Why would you want to go there?" asked an old lady a little way down the road.

"Why not!" the three friends answered together.

"You can't travel to the end of the world. Nobody has ever been there," warned a crossing guard when he discovered their plan. "I forbid you to cross here!"

"Or else what?" asked Trik.

"Or else . . . there will be consequences!" said the guard.

But Zip, Trik, and Flip crossed anyway.

The three friends walked and walked until they reached a huge expanse of water.

"So, is this where the world ends?" asked Zip.
"I think so," answered Trik.
"It looks a bit flat, doesn't it," observed Flip.

But then they saw a small boat approaching from far away.

The three friends climbed aboard.

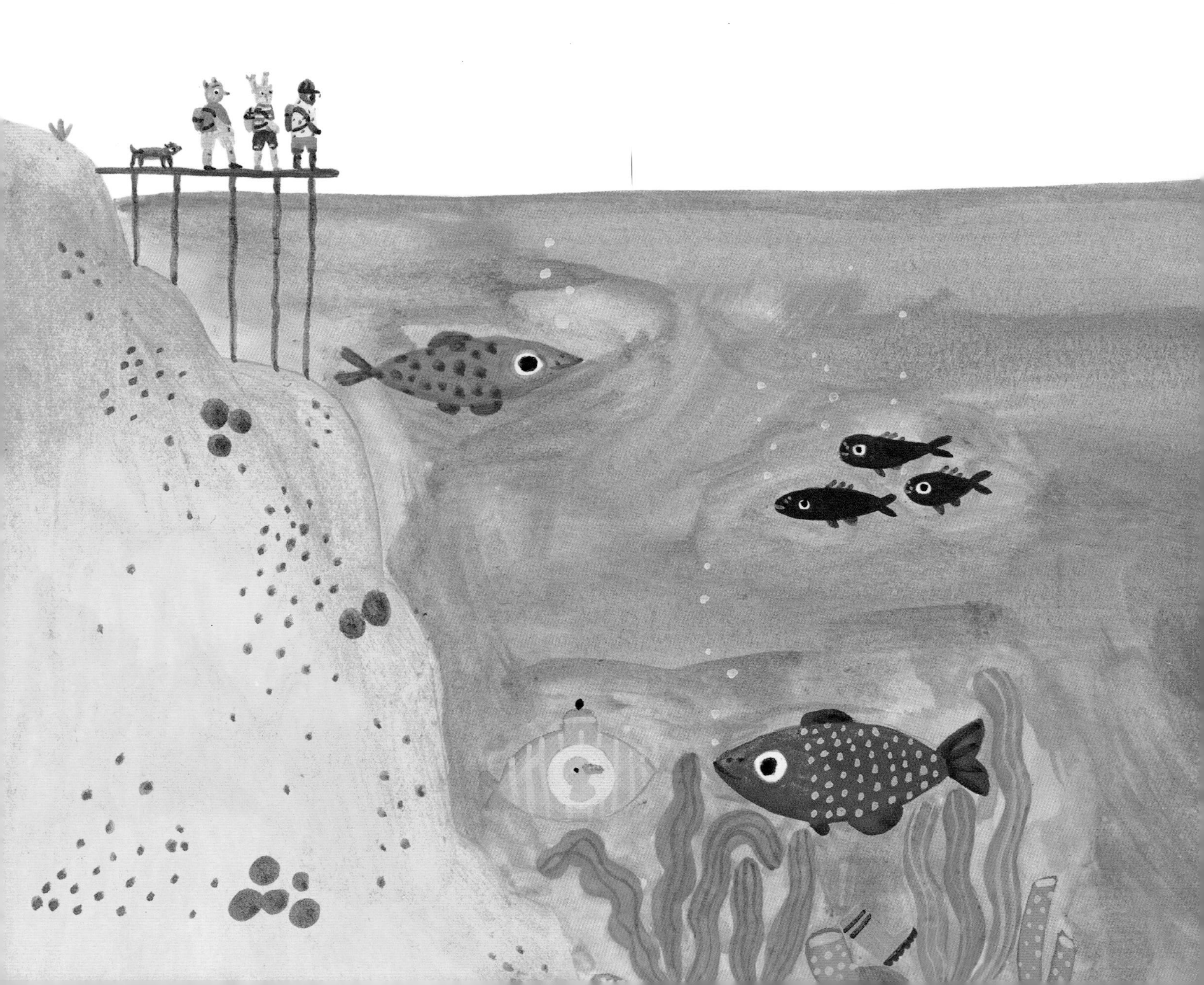

"Can you take us to where the world ends?" asked Zip.
"No, but I can bring you to the other side of the lake," replied the boatman.

And so they went.

They reached the opposite shore and went on searching, asking for directions from everyone they met.

Someone said that the end of the world was at the peak of a nearby mountain.

But once they got
there, they were
told that the end
of the world was at
the bottom of the
next valley.

Once they reached
the valley, someone
pointed them toward
a meadow.

And when they crossed the meadow, they were told that the end of the world was, for sure, on the other side of the forest.

They were also told that it was
impossible to cross the forest.

The three friends made it out of the woods and kept walking,
marching over hill after windswept hill.

But the world still seemed to continue, so they kept on going.

A nosey onlooker said that it was silly
to try and find the end of the world.
Zip, Trik, and Flip didn’t mind what anyone else thought.

But every time they came closer to the end
of the world, it seemed to move farther away.

At the top of a distant hill, they finally saw it.

"*Ooh!*" they all said together. "So, is that where the world ends?"

After catching their breath, they turned around and headed home. They knew they would have a long way to go.

Luckily, they still had some peanuts for the journey.

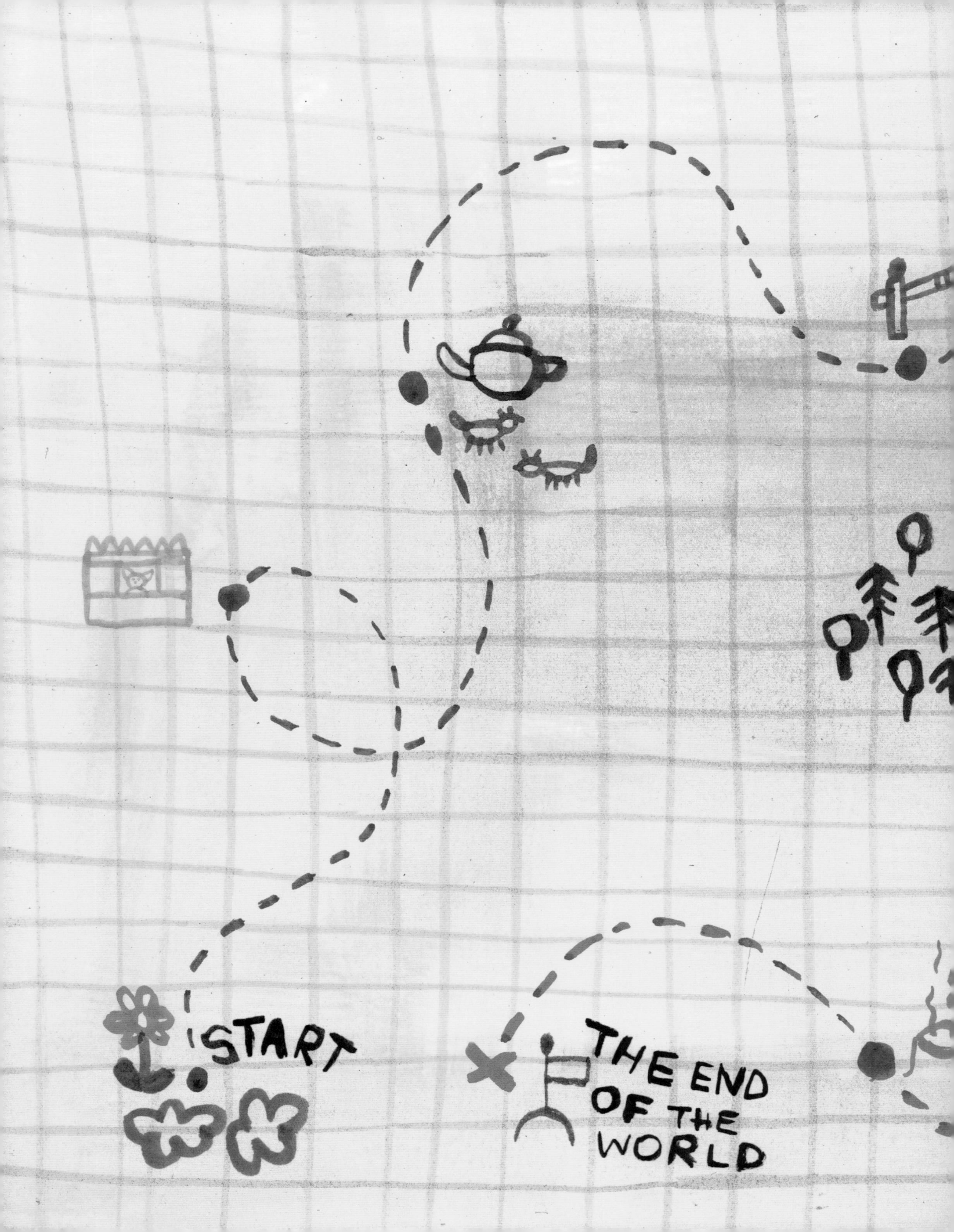
START
THE END OF THE WORLD